WHERE'S LARRY?

Philip Barrett

THE O'BRIEN PRESS
DUBLIN

WHERE'S LARRY?

Come on a unique, exciting tour of Ireland with Larry the Leprechaun. He's lived here a very long time, so he knows all the best and most famous places around the country.

As you will know, leprechauns are small fellows and special to Ireland, but they're very hard to spot. They each have a crock of gold and their main aim in life is to stop humans grabbing it! They usually hide it at the end of a rainbow (try finding THAT!). You must not get on the wrong side of a leprechaun or he will make things very uncomfortable for you. So keep your wits about you on this tour!

Larry likes to hide, anyway, so he won't bother you if you don't bother him. Your job is simply to FIND him! He's small – and he can hide very well. But he does wear a distinctive outfit.

Hello there! I'm Larry the Leprechaun. I hear you're going to be following me all around Ireland. I'm not sure I like that. We leprechauns hate to be spotted by humans. Anyway, I bet you won't be able to find ME. There are lots of 'friends' and other things following me around too. They're everywhere! You can spot THEM if you wish (they *do* change their clothes – and even their gender!).

HELP ME FIND MY FRIENDS:

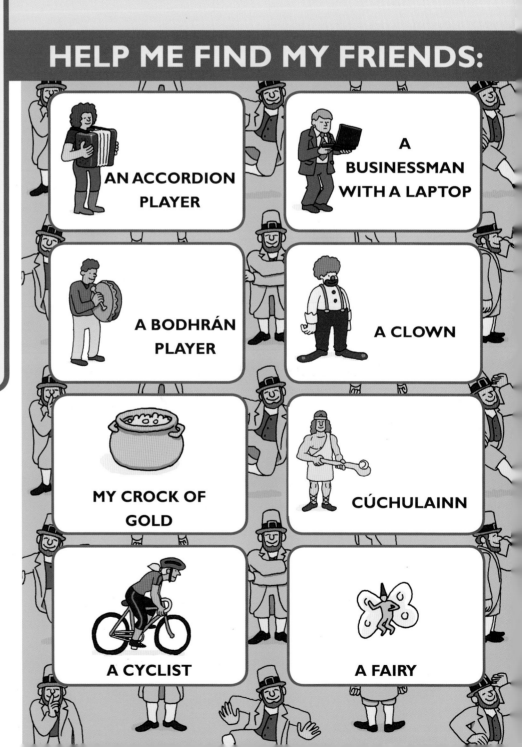

AN ACCORDION PLAYER

A BUSINESSMAN WITH A LAPTOP

A BODHRÁN PLAYER

A CLOWN

MY CROCK OF GOLD

CÚCHULAINN

A CYCLIST

A FAIRY

THE CLIFFS OF MOHER A fine windy place to start our circuit of Ireland. These are the highest and steepest cliffs in the whole country. They're up to 214m high and 8km long. Don't go too near the edge! Every so often there's a HUGE wave off the coast here and surfers – really good surfers – try out their skills on it. But don't try it yourself, now! That's the Atlantic, and it is big and cold and dangerous. You're looking at America out there, you know (even if you can't actually see it). Now, can you see ME? I hope not. And, even more important, can you see me crock of gold? I'm watching you!

GALWAY BAY This regatta is great fun altogether. I love regattas and I go to loads of them every year all around the country. But I like the ones with old boats best. The oldest boats in Galway are called 'hookers' (I swear). They're the black boats with the red sails. They're great on the windy seas around here with their one big sail and two small ones in front. But there are loads of different boats in the bay today. That's because it's a really sunny day (for Ireland) and everyone wants to be on the water. Including ME!

GALWAY 1

4502 USA

CROAGH PATRICK Now, this is a very strange place – the holiest mountain in Ireland. Every year in July people come here and climb to the top. Some of them take off their shoes to do it! I don't understand that at all – I do it in comfort, meself. There's a fantastic view – there are supposed to be 365 islands in the bay, one for every day of the year! The annual climb is all in memory of St Patrick who climbed this very mountain in the fifth century. But it was a holy mountain even before St Patrick, you know. I remember it from pagan times and I know all the best hiding places. Hah!

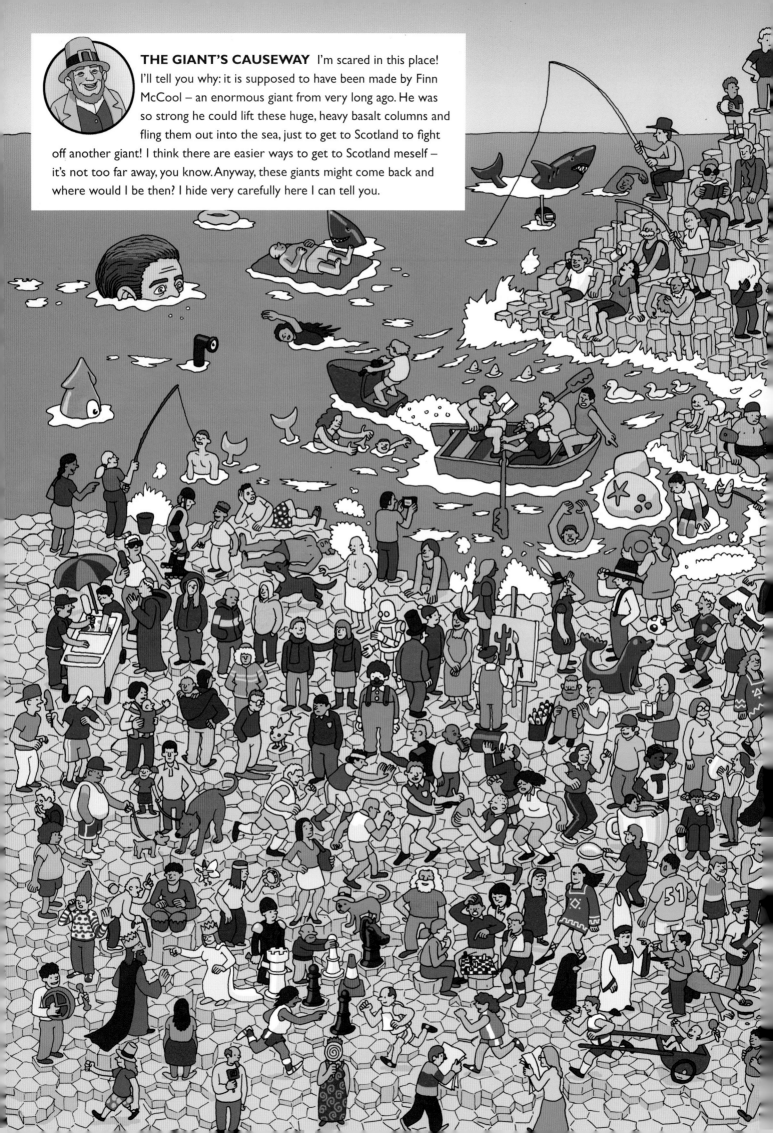

THE GIANT'S CAUSEWAY I'm scared in this place! I'll tell you why: it is supposed to have been made by Finn McCool – an enormous giant from very long ago. He was so strong he could lift these huge, heavy basalt columns and fling them out into the sea, just to get to Scotland to fight off another giant! I think there are easier ways to get to Scotland meself – it's not too far away, you know. Anyway, these giants might come back and where would I be then? I hide very carefully here I can tell you.

NEWGRANGE We're really talking OLD here. This place is as old as ME! The mound was made about five thousand years ago as a burial place. And there's a great trick here: at the winter solstice in December sunlight shines through a channel into the INSIDE of the hill and lights up a chamber there. I watched them working on all that – it took a lot of figuring out, I tell you. Now, where's me crock of gold? I hope it's not inside in that hill …

CROKE PARK This is the pitch where they play the All-Ireland finals in Gaelic football and hurling. Now, those are great days altogether. The place is full to the brim with people wearing their county colours and roaring their heads off. I'd say that giant Cúchulainn is thrilled to be HERE. He's very good at hurling, you know. He could be a whole team all by himself. I'd better keep an eye on him – or he'll sneak off with me crock of gold on his hurley.

ST PATRICK'S DAY PARADE This is O'Connell Street, Dublin, outside the GPO on St Patrick's Day, 17 March. It's mad altogether. Them bands make a fierce racket even in this wide street – I can see why those fellas are trying to climb the Spire to get away from it (I hope they don't slip down!). The thing I don't like is the snakey thing – St Patrick drove them fellas out, you know, and here he is again trying to get rid of the very last one, it seems. Is his work never done? I'm not sure about that flying fella either – he must be able to see everything from up there. Hmm!

COLLEGE GREEN This is in the middle of Dublin city. There's Trinity College on the right, where you can go and see the Book of Kells. And the building on the left is the old parliament building – Ireland was (sort of) ruled from there up to 1800, when it was closed down. I remember it well – all those lords arriving on their horses to make the laws. Very grand it was. Now the place is full of noise – cars and buses driving by all the time. I'm a bit scared of it, to tell you the truth. Full of chancers too, so I've hidden me stuff and meself very carefully.

GLENDALOUGH I know this place since that fella Kevin built his monastery here in the fifth century. He used to get up at all hours and sing with his monks. It was lovely chanty music. Every three hours they did it. You wouldn't get any sleep here at all. But they were very kind and left out food for the birds and animals (and the leprechauns, though they didn't actually know that!). The mountains here are great for hiking (or hiding) in.

THE ROCK OF CASHEL The kings of Munster used to live here in the old days. I remember how it was then, full of feasting and hunting and battles. It was great fun altogether. It's up on a high hill looking out over the whole country so that they knew when danger was coming. I remember Brian Boru living here in the tenth century – he was the strongest king ever. He died after the Battle of Clontarf in 1014. I was very sad because we all had a good time while he ruled Ireland. There's a round tower here too, so if you missed the one in Glendalough, now's your chance.

VOTE

KEEP CLOSED

PUCK FAIR, KILLORGLIN I'd be wary of those wild goats, if I were you. That fella up there on his perch – he's dangerous. I know, because I've been coming to Puck Fair since it began – and that was over two thousand years ago at least. I've seen lots of them wild goats. One of them nearly got me crock of gold once, the scoundrel. I had to climb up and grab it in front of everyone. 'Twas a wonder I got away with it. Them goats like hats and scarves and bags too, so hold onto your stuff!

BUNRATTY CASTLE We're finished our circuit of Ireland and back in County Clare. A castle was first built here hundreds of years ago by the Normans. It was burned down a lot because everybody wanted to own it and they all fought over it, so they had to rebuild it many times. This 'new' castle was built in 1425. Now it is full of old furniture and things. I often sneak in and have a lie-down on one of those lovely beds. They're just the right size for me. Humans weren't that much bigger than me in the old days, though now they're huge. Bet you can't find me and me gold here! It's your last chance.

THE WHERE'S LARRY? CHECKLISTS

Lots more things for Larry watchers to look for!

The Cliffs of Moher

- [ ] a frog on a lily pad
- [ ] a cowboy in the wind
- [ ] a puffin puffing on a pipe
- [ ] a bird on tv and a bird on a tv
- [ ] a star on a sinking boat
- [ ] a sea serpent
- [ ] 2 barrels and a treasure chest
- [ ] a high diver and a diving seagull
- [ ] a hot-dog stand
- [ ] a half-covered danger sign
- [ ] 4 ducks and a rubber duck
- [ ] a bird with a crown
- [ ] a spider robot
- [ ] a snorkeller

Galway Bay

- [ ] a dolphin
- [ ] a donkey
- [ ] a Viking in a Viking boat
- [ ] a clown boat
- [ ] a 'banana' boat
- [ ] a giant lobster
- [ ] 2 jetskis
- [ ] a tortoise
- [ ] a swimmer pretending to be a shark
- [ ] 2 cooks arguing
- [ ] a yawning man
- [ ] a sail mender
- [ ] 3 top hats in a top hat
- [ ] a windsurfer
- [ ] an owl and a pussycat in a pea-green boat

Croagh Patrick

- [ ] walking sticks for sale
- [ ] shoes for sale
- [ ] a snail
- [ ] a spotted dog
- [ ] a pogo stick
- [ ] a boxer
- [ ] a crashed hang glider

- [ ] a donkey
- [ ] a 3-legged walk and a 4-legged walk
- [ ] a bird with a walking stick
- [ ] 3 parachutists
- [ ] a zombie walker
- [ ] a hula-hooper

The Giant's Causeway

- ☐ a giant teacup
- ☐ a penguin
- ☐ a bongo player
- ☐ a black cat
- ☐ a Viking boat
- ☐ 2 ballet dancers
- ☐ a shark
- ☐ a starfish
- ☐ a fish in a net
- ☐ a vampire
- ☐ a fish with feet
- ☐ a t-shirt with a T
- ☐ a giant handbag
- ☐ a road cone as a hat

Newgrange

- ☐ a dog doing Irish dancing
- ☐ a giant ice-cream
- ☐ fake rain
- ☐ a man in a catsuit
- ☐ a frightened runner
- ☐ a baseball player
- ☐ a dog stealing some chicken
- ☐ a body builder
- ☐ a nosey newspaper reader
- ☐ 2 jugglers
- ☐ a skateboarder
- ☐ a barbecue
- ☐ a baby with a rattler
- ☐ falling acrobats
- ☐ sunglasses in the passage

Croke Park

- ☐ a fat cat
- ☐ a drink being spilt
- ☐ a rock band
- ☐ the start of a Mexican wave
- ☐ a sombrero
- ☐ a big head
- ☐ 3 fish in the net
- ☐ a chef
- ☐ 3 tall hats
- ☐ 'Shakespeare'
- ☐ a witch's flag
- ☐ a robot
- ☐ a man trying to get on telly
- ☐ an alien

St Patrick's Day Parade

- ☐ a big fried egg
- ☐ a kung fu fighter
- ☐ a big man who's lost his head
- ☐ a big head that's lost its pipe
- ☐ someone dressed as a big shamrock
- ☐ a cow chasing grass
- ☐ monkeys on a big banana
- ☐ a man using tall hats to get a view
- ☐ birds attacking a bird man
- ☐ a garda turned into a frog
- ☐ a mobile DJ
- ☐ a snake charmer
- ☐ 2 koala bears

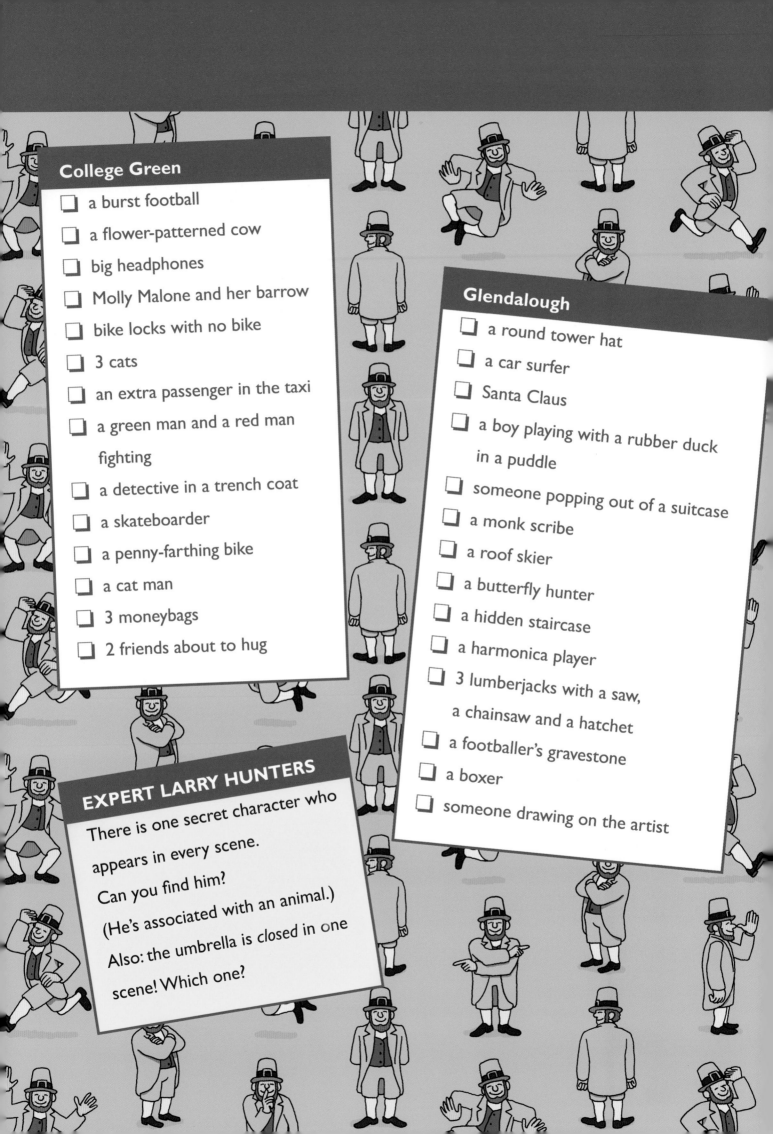

College Green

- [ ] a burst football
- [ ] a flower-patterned cow
- [ ] big headphones
- [ ] Molly Malone and her barrow
- [ ] bike locks with no bike
- [ ] 3 cats
- [ ] an extra passenger in the taxi
- [ ] a green man and a red man fighting
- [ ] a detective in a trench coat
- [ ] a skateboarder
- [ ] a penny-farthing bike
- [ ] a cat man
- [ ] 3 moneybags
- [ ] 2 friends about to hug

Glendalough

- [ ] a round tower hat
- [ ] a car surfer
- [ ] Santa Claus
- [ ] a boy playing with a rubber duck in a puddle
- [ ] someone popping out of a suitcase
- [ ] a monk scribe
- [ ] a roof skier
- [ ] a butterfly hunter
- [ ] a hidden staircase
- [ ] a harmonica player
- [ ] 3 lumberjacks with a saw, a chainsaw and a hatchet
- [ ] a footballer's gravestone
- [ ] a boxer
- [ ] someone drawing on the artist

EXPERT LARRY HUNTERS

There is one secret character who appears in every scene. Can you find him? (He's associated with an animal.) Also: the umbrella is *closed* in one scene! Which one?

The Rock of Cashel

- [ ] a rock band
- [ ] happy and sad backpacks
- [ ] rollerskater taking a rest
- [ ] a flying saucer
- [ ] a climbing spider
- [ ] a blue woodpecker
- [ ] a matador
- [ ] Little Red Riding Hood
- [ ] someone wearing a red hoodie
- [ ] the sword in the stone
- [ ] 2 rabbits
- [ ] Rapunzel
- [ ] a telescope
- [ ] badminton players
- [ ] a shamrock on a cow

Puck Fair, Killorglin

- [ ] a golfer
- [ ] a hobby-horse
- [ ] a horse-shaped balloon
- [ ] a banjo player
- [ ] a dog taking a man for a walk
- [ ] the mystery box stall
- [ ] a broken crystal ball
- [ ] 2 sleeping bags
- [ ] a giant carrot
- [ ] a donkey carrying turf
- [ ] 3 dropped ice-cream cones
- [ ] a tightrope walker
- [ ] a sausage dog

Bunratty Castle

- [ ] an octopus tentacle with a phone
- [ ] an electric car
- [ ] a giant suitcase
- [ ] juggling hands
- [ ] 2 remote-control cars
- [ ] someone hiding in a bush
- [ ] a giant blue egg
- [ ] a girl boxer

- [ ] a high diver
- [ ] a large letter
- [ ] a bungee jumper
- [ ] a castle-shaped tent
- [ ] a witch stuck in a window
- [ ] the king and queen
- [ ] king and queen birds

First published 2012

by The O'Brien Press Ltd,

12 Terenure Road East,

Dublin 6, D06 HD27, Ireland.

Tel: +353 1 4923333

Fax: +353 1 4922777

E-mail: books@obrien.ie

Website: obrien.ie

Reprinted 2013, 2015, 2016, 2017, 2018, 2019, 2022 (twice).

The O'Brien Press is a member of

Publishing Ireland.

ISBN: 978-1-84717-276-1

Copyright for illustrations © Philip Barrett

The moral rights of the author have been asserted.

Copyright for text, editing, layout & design © The O'Brien Press Ltd.

11 10 9

24 23 22

Printed and bound in Poland by Białostockie Zakłady Graficzne S.A.

The paper used in this book is produced using pulp from managed forests.

Where's Larry? received financial assistance from the Arts Council.

the arts council chomhairle ealaíon | funding literature

Growing up with O'BRIEN obrien.ie

Published in:
DUBLIN
UNESCO
City of Literature